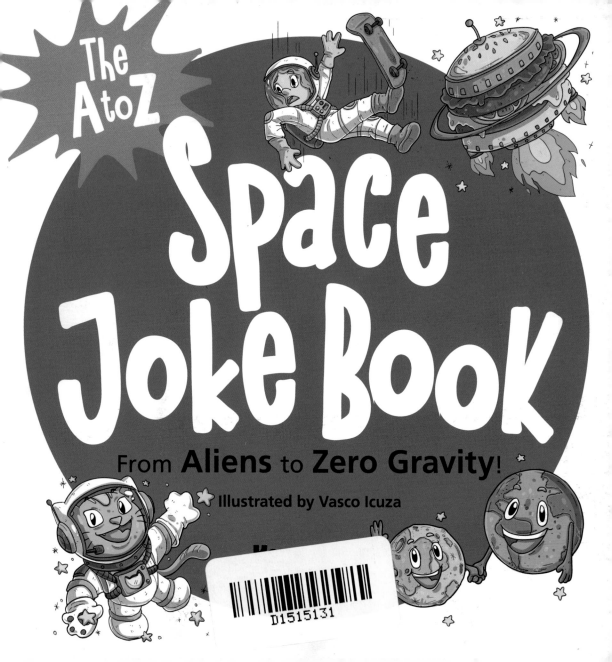

# The A to Z

# Space Joke Book

## From **Aliens** to **Zero Gravity**!

Illustrated by Vasco Icuza

BWAHAHA!
HA HA!
CHORTLE!
HAHAHA!
HE HE!
CACKLE!
TEE-HEE!
LOL!
GIGGLE!
HAH!

# The A to Z Space Joke Book

**If your sense of humor is otherworldly**,
and you love nothing more than making others laugh,
then you'll be over the moon with this book!

*The A to Z Space Joke Book* is an out-of-this-world
collection of over 300 space-themed one-liners.
The jokes are ordered alphabetically, so you can chuckle
your way from A to Z, or search for a joke about your
favorite space object. From an amusing atmosphere to
the zany zero gravity, the laughs don't stop!

*The A to Z Space Joke Book* will really send
your friends and family into orbit!

**Q** How did the astronauts cause an **ACCIDENT**?

**A** It was getting stuffy in the rocket, so they rolled down a window!

**Q** How did the astronaut **ACCIDENTLY** break his phone?

**A** He Saturn it!

**Q** Why can't most people **AFFORD** a trip to the Moon?

**A** Because the prices are *astro*nomical!

**Q** Why is the Moon never **AFRAID**?

**A** Because it lacks atmos-fear!

**Q** Why is there no **AIR** in space?

**A** So that the Milky Way doesn't go bad!

SNICKER!

**Q** What do you do when **ALIENS** get angry?

**A** You give them some space!

**Q** What was the first **ANIMAL** in space?

**A** The cow that jumped over the Moon!

**Q** What do you call an astronaut that **ANSWERS** back?

**A** A sass-tronaut!

**Q** What does space-time travel have in common with **APPLES**?

**A** Wormholes!

**Q** What did one rocket scientist say to the other during an **ARGUMENT**?

**A** "Let me atom!"

GUFFAW!

**Q** Did you hear about the new fruit spread with tiny pieces of **ASTEROID** in it?

**A** It's called space jam!

**Q** What do **ASTRONAUTS** do when they get angry?

**A** They blast off!

**Q** What does an **ASTRONOMER** do with bubble gum?

**A** Blow Hubbles!

**Q** What do you call pastries outside of a planet's **ATMOSPHERE**?

**A** Space-tries!

**Q** Why are **ATOMS** considered the most untrustworthy things in the universe?

**A** Because they make up everything!

TEE-HEE!

**Q** What did the astronauts call their **BABY**?

**A** Inter-stella!

**Q** What do you call a comet wrapped in **BACON**?

**A** A meat-eor!

**Q** What's the Moon's favorite kind of **BAGEL**?

**A** Cinna-moon raisin!

**Q** What do you call an astronaut's **BEARD**?

**A** Spatial hair!

BWAHAHA!

**Q** What do you call a professional who tries to make space look even more **BEAUTIFUL**?

**A** A cosmo-tologist!

**Q** What do astronauts wear to **BED**?

**A** Space jammies!

**Q** What **BEE** went into space?

**A** Buzz Aldrin!

**Q** Why shouldn't you ask a busy scientist what existed before the **BIG BANG**?

**A** They'll just say there's no time!

**Q** How did the astronaut react to the **BIRTHDAY** present he received?

**A** He was over the moon!

HA HA!

**Q** Why don't aliens celebrate **BIRTHDAYS**?

**A** Because they don't like to give away their presence!

**Q** How did the **BLACK HOLE** lose so much weight?

**A** It ate light!

**Q** What did the astronauts say when they found **BONES** on the Moon?

**A** "Guess the cow didn't make it!"

**Q** Did you hear about the new **BOOK** all about antigravity?

**A** It's impossible to put down!

**Q** What's the difference between an alien and a loaf of **BREAD**?

**A** You don't know? Well, I'm not sending *you* to the bakery, then!

**Q** What is the Moon's favorite **BREAKFAST** food?

**A** Crescent rolls!

HAHAHA!

**Q** What's round, **BRIGHT**, and silly?

**A** A fool moon!

**Q** What happened to the astronauts who **BROKE** the laws of gravity?

**A** They got suspended sentences!

**Q** What's **BROWN**, hairy, and goes into space?

**A** A coco-naut!

**Q** What kind of space scientist puts **BUBBLES** in lemonade?

**A** An astro-*fizz*-icist!

**Q** What do you get if you cross a **BURGER** with a space shuttle?

**A** Very, very, fast food!

**C**

**Q** What do you **CALL** a galaxy that's allergic to milk?

**A** Ga-lactose intolerant!

**Q** Why are astronauts always so **CALM**?

**A** Because there is no pressure in space!

**Q** What do a movie **CAMERA OPERATOR** and an astronomer have in common?

**A** Both their jobs involve shooting stars!

**Q** What do aliens love to ride at the space **CARNIVAL**?

**A** The solar coaster!

**Q** Who in the solar system has the most loose **CHANGE**?

**A** The Moon—it keeps changing quarters!

TEE-HEE!

**Q** What space **CHANNEL** should you watch on TV if you want to laugh?

**A** The comet-y channel!

**Q** What do you call a **CHICKEN** from outer space?

**A** An egg-stra-terrestrial!

**Q** What do you call a **CHILLY** space traveler?

**A** An ice-tronaut!

CHORTLE!

**Q** What's the alien **CHOIR'S** favorite song to sing?

**A** "Amazing Space"!

**Q** What do you call a planet that tastes like **CITRUS**?

**A** *Le*moon!

**Q** What do Martians study in music **CLASS**?

**A** Big band theory!

**Q** Why should you never look at an eclipse through a **COLANDER**?

**A** You'll strain your eyes!

**Q** Where do alien **COMEDIANS** come from?

**A** Planet of the japes!

**Q** Why was the **COMET** so good at playing basketball?

**A** Because it was a shooting star!

**Q** What's an astronaut's favorite part of a **COMPUTER**?

**A** The space bar!

GIGGLE!

**Q** How do you throw the best music **CONCERT** in space?

**A** You rocket!

SNICKER!

**Q** What did the alien **CONFESS** to the astronaut?

**A** "I used to love time travel, but that's all in the past now!"

**Q** How is Sagittarius distinct from other **CONSTELLATIONS**?

**A** It is the centaur of attention!

**Q** How do aliens **COUNT** to seventeen?

**A** On their fingers!

**Q** Why did the **COW** go to outer space?

**A** To visit the Milky Way!

**Q** Which planet did the aliens **CRASH** into?

**A** Splat-urn!

**Q** What did the astronauts do after they **CRASHED** into the Moon?

**A** They Apollo-gized!

**Q** What do you say to a three-headed space **CREATURE**?

**A** "Hello! Hello! Hello!"

**Q** Which **CREEPY-CRAWLY** refuses to ever go into space?

**A** The earthworm!

**Q** Why do aliens make **CROP CIRCLES**?

**A** Because they're corny!

GUFFAW!

**Q** What **DANCE** do all astronauts know?

**A** The moonwalk!

**Q** What really makes an astronaut's **DAY**?

**A** The Sun's rotation!

**Q** What did the astronaut say to his **DENTIST**?

**A** "I've got a black hole!"

**Q** What makes up a large portion of an alien's **DIET**?

**A** Unidentified frying objects!

**Q** Why are some astronauts so **DIFFICULT** to talk to?

**A** They're just not down-to-earth!

**Q** How do astronomers make **DISCOVERIES**?

**A** By cos-mosis!

**Q** What did the astronaut say to the **DOCTOR** just before takeoff?

**A** Time to get my booster shot!

HAW-HAW!

**Q** Why did Jupiter see so many **DOCTORS**?

**A** Because it had a big, red spot that wouldn't go away!

**Q** Why doesn't the **DOG STAR** laugh at jokes?

**A** It's far too Sirius!

**Q** Why do **DOGS** hate being in outer space?

**A** Because they are afraid of vacuums!

**Q** Did you hear that someone paid 10,000 **DOLLARS** to send a cat into space?

**A** It was a cat-astro-fee!

**Q** Which hot **DRINK** do all Martians love?

**A** Gravi-tea!

**Q** What do astronauts serve **DRINKS** in?

**A** Sunglasses!

GIGGLE!

**Q** What do astronauts use to **DUST** black holes?

**A** Vacuum cleaners!

**Q** Which **DWARF PLANET** might show some signs of life?

**A** Scientists believe Pluto may have fleas!

**Q** What do you call an alien who has no **EARS**?

**A** Anything you like—it can't hear you!

**Q** What is **EARTH'S** worst habit?

**A** Making fun of other planets for having no life!

**Q** What did the Sun say when it reappeared after an **ECLIPSE**?

**A** "Pleased to heat you again!"

**Q** How does the solar system like its **EGGS** cooked?

**A** Sunny-side up!

**Q** Which day of the week is a NASA **ENGINEER'S** favorite day?

**A** Fly-day!

WA HA HA

**Q** Why did the astrophysicists **EXCAVATE** the field?

**A** They were searching for wormholes!

**Q** What is the Sun's favorite way to **EXERCISE**?

**A** On the solar cycle!

GUFFAW!

**Q** What do astronauts say when asked to **EXPLAIN** what they enjoy about the job?

**A** "It has its ups and downs!"

**Q** What did the **EXTRATERRESTRIAL** say to his friend after a long time apart?

**A** "Jupiter recognize me, or else!"

**Q** What is an alien with three **EYES** called?

**A** An aliiien!

**Q** When do astronauts **FALL** off their skateboards?

**A** When they lose ground control!

**Q** What's the best board game to play with your **FAMILY** in space?

**A** Moon-opoly!

**Q** What's the most **FAMOUS** painting of an eclipse?

**A** The Moon-a Lisa!

**Q** What is the **FARTHEST** you can travel for free?

**A** Around the Sun—and you do it every year!

**Q** What is **FAST**, loud, and crunchy?

**A** A rocket chip!

HAH!

**F**

CACKLE!

**Q** What's an alien's **FAVORITE** day of the week?

**A** Sunday!

**Q** What do you call a **FELINE** orbiting in outer space?

**A** A cat-ellite!

**Q** What do you call it when two stars have a **FIGHT**?

**A** Star wars!

**Q** Do Martians eat popcorn with their **FINGERS**?

**A** No, they eat the fingers separately!

**Q** What type of **FISH** do you find in space?

**A** Starfish!

**Q** Why is it impossible that Earth is **FLAT**?

**A** Because if it was, cats would have pushed everything off its edge by now!

**Q** What did the space travelers eat on their **FLIGHT**?

**A** Astro-nuts!

**Q** What type of **FLOWERS** grow on the surface of the Sun?

**A** Ultraviolets!

**Q** Why couldn't the astronauts **FOCUS**?

**A** They kept spacing out!

TEE-HEE!

**Q** Where do astronauts keep their space **FOOD**?

**A** In their launch boxes!

**Q** Why don't astronauts like **FOOTBALL**?

**A** They prefer liftoffs to touchdowns!

CHORTLE!

**Q** Why are aliens so **FORGETFUL**?

**A** Because everything goes in one ear and out two others!

**Q** How do we know that Earth is a **FRIEND** of the Moon?

**A** We've seen them hanging around together for years!

**Q** Why is Earth not **FRIENDS** with the Sun?

**A** Because the Sun thinks it is above everyone else!

**Q** Which is heavier, a **FULL** moon or a half-moon?

**A** A half-moon — a full moon is lighter!

**Q** What did the alien say to the **GARDEN**?

**A** "Take me to your weeder!"

HAHAHA!

**Q** Why are Martians such good **GARDENERS**?

**A** They have green fingers!

**Q** What kind of stars wear **GLASSES**?

**A** Movie stars!

**Q** Why did the astronaut want to play **GOLF** in outer space?

**A** She wanted to get a black-hole-in-one!

**Q** Why are aliens **GREEN**?

**A** They always forget to take their space-sickness pills!

**Q** How does Earth's Sun get a **HAIRCUT**?

**A** Eclipse it!

**Q** What happened when the astronomer hit his **HEAD** on the telescope?

**A** He was seeing stars for days!

**Q** Why couldn't the astronaut put her **HELMET** on?

**A** She didn't have enough space!

**Q** Why is the Moon more **HELPFUL** than the Sun?

**A** Because we really need the light at night!

HA HA!

**Q** What device helps scientists collect futuristic **HERBS**?

**A** A thyme machine!

**Q** What did the vegan Black **HOLE** say?

**A** "I'm on a strictly planet-based diet!"

**Q** Why couldn't the astronaut book a **HOTEL** room on the Moon?

**A** Because it was full!

**Q** What happened when the astronomers got tired of watching the Moon go around the Earth for 24 **HOURS**?

**A** They called it a day!

LOL!

**Q** Why do you have to clean your **HOUSE** so much in space?

**A** Stardust is everywhere!

**Q** Why aren't astronauts **HUNGRY** when they get to space?

**A** They always have a big launch right before!

**Q** How do astronauts eat their **ICE CREAM**?

**A** In floats!

**Q** What did the **INEXPERIENCED** astronauts think of their first takeoff?

**A** They thought it was a blast!

HA HA!

**Q** Why aren't jokes about **INFINITY** funny?

**A** They never end!

**Q** Why do astronauts feel **INSECURE**?

**A** Their jobs are always up in the air!

**Q** What sort of saddle would you put on an **INTERGALACTIC** horse?

**A** A saddle-lite!

**Q** Why do astronauts love the cafeteria on the **INTERNATIONAL SPACE STATION** so much?

**A** Because the food is out of this world!

**Q** Did you hear about the astronaut who did well in **INTERVIEWS**?

**A** She was great at landing a job!

**Q** What did the alien **INVADER** say to the cat?

**A** "Take me to your litter!"

**Q** Will **INVISIBLE** spaceships ever happen?

**A** No, I don't think they will take off!

**Q** Do you know why you never see a meteor by **ITSELF**?

**A** Because they travel im*pacts*!

LOL!

# J

**Q** Why did the asteroid quit its **JOB** and move to LA?

**A** It wanted to be a stand-up comet!

**Q** How do astronauts describe their **JOBS**?

**A** As "heavenly"!

**Q** Why did the grown-up planet **JOIN** the solar system?

**A** It had always wanted a Sun!

**Q** Why did the cow **JUMP** over the Moon?

**A** The farmer had really cold hands!

**Q** Did you know that **JUPITER** has a total of 64 moons?

**A** Their werewolf problem must be out of this world!

**Q** What do you get when you cross a space alien and a **KANGAROO**?

**A** A *Mars*upial!

**Q** What happens when astronauts break a **KEY** on their laptops?

**A** They lose ctrl!

**Q** Why did the **KIDS** think that they would never become successful astronauts?

**A** Because their parents told them, "The sky's the limit!"

**Q** What **KIND** of bond does the Sun have with all the planets in its solar system?

**A** A bond of *so*lidarity!

HE HE!

**Q** How do you **KNOW** if an alien has been in your refrigerator?

**A** There are footprints in the butter!

**Q** What do you get when you cross a **LAMB** and a rocket?

**A** A space sheep!

**Q** What did the meteorite say when it **LANDED**?

**A** "I think I just hit rock bottom!"

**Q** What did Neil Armstrong say when no one **LAUGHED** at his Moon jokes?

**A** "I guess you had to be there!"

**Q** What do you call a potato that has been **LAUNCHED** into space?

**A** A Spud-nik!

GIGGLE!

**Q** What do you call a **LAZY** person in space?

**A** A pro-cras-tronaut!

**Q** Did you hear the **LECTURE** about Halley's Comet?

**A** It went completely over my head!

**Q** What did the **LIBRARIAN** say to the astronaut?

**A** "Find space for a book!"

**Q** Who wrote the book *My **LIFE** in Outer Space*?

**A** I. Malone!

**Q** How many astronomers does it take to change a **LIGHT BULB**?

**A** None! They are always happy in the dark!

**Q** What's a **LIGHT-YEAR**?

**A** It's like a regular year, but with fewer calories!

**L**

**Q** Why didn't the customers **LIKE** the restaurant on the Moon?

**A** Because there was no atmosphere!

**Q** What is the fastest **LIQUID** in the universe?

**A** Milk — pasteurized before you see it!

**Q** Why does the Moon raise and **LOWER** the tides over and over again?

**A** Just to make shore!

CHUCKLE!

**Q** On which day of the week does the **LUNAR ECLIPSE** happen?

**A** Moon-day!

**Q** What do you call the headlights on a **LUNAR ROVER**?

**A** Moonbeams!

**Q** How did the astronomer calculate the Moon's **MAGNETIC** field?

**A** He used inductive reasoning!

**Q** What do aliens do after they get **MARRIED**?

**A** Go on a honey-earth!

**Q** What did **MARS** say to Saturn?

**A** "Give me a ring sometime!"

**Q** What kind of fur do you get from a **MARTIAN**?

**A** As fur away as possible!

**Q** How do astronauts heat their **MEALS**?

**A** With a space heater!

TEE-HEE!

**Q** What did one **METEOR** say to the other?

**A** "You rock my world!"

**Q** What did the asteroid say to the **METEOROID**?

**A** "You're a chip off the old block!"

**Q** What do you get if a **MICROSCOPE** crashes into a telescope?

**A** A collide-oscope!

**Q** What do a bag of potato chips and the **MILKY WAY** have in common?

**A** They're both mostly empty space!

BWAHAHA!

**Q** If a meteor becomes a meteorite once it hits Earth, what do you call a meteor that **MISSES** Earth?

**A** A meteor-left!

**Q** What is **MONEY** called in space?

**A** Star bucks!

**Q** What should you do if you see a blue space **MONSTER**?

**A** Try to cheer him up!

**Q** Why is the Moon constantly **MOODY**?

**A** It's just going through a phase!

**Q** How do you know when the **MOON** has had enough to eat?

**A** When it's full!

**Q** What do you call a meal cooked on the **MOON'S** surface?

**A** A satellite dish!

**Q** What did the Martian's **MOTHER** say when it got home from its travels?

**A** "Where on Earth have you been?"

**Q** Why did the aliens have to **MOVE** to a new house?

**A** They were outer space!

**Q** What is Saturn's favorite **MOVIE**?

**A** *Lord of the Rings*!

**Q** What is an astronaut's favorite type of **MUSIC**?

**A** Space rock!

**Q** Why don't people like to talk about all the **MYSTERIOUS** space in the universe?

**A** It's a dark matter!

CACKLE!

**Q** How do astronauts **NAP**?

**A** They drift off!

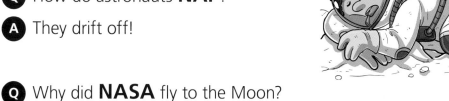

**Q** Why did **NASA** fly to the Moon?

**A** Because it was too far to walk!

**Q** What happens when astronauts are **NAUGHTY**?

**A** They get grounded!

**Q** Did you hear about the party on **NEPTUNE**?

**A** It was a gas!

HAHAHA!

**Q** Why is the Sun **NEVER** on time for anything?

**A** It is always fashionably light!

**Q** What did the alien say to the **NEWS** reporter?

**A** "No comet!"

**Q** What do astronauts use to see at **NIGHT**?

**A** Satellites!

**Q** What does **NITROGEN** become when the Sun rises?

**A** Day-trogen!

**Q** Who wrote the **NOVEL** *Proof of Extraterrestrials*?

**A** A. Leon Being!

**Q** What type of weekend trips do **NUCLEAR** scientists take?

**A** Fission trips!

HE HE!

**Q** What is the largest **OCEAN** in space?

**A** The Galex Sea!

SNICKER!

**Q** What happens if an astronaut **OPENS** a window during takeoff?

**A** They have their head in the clouds for a while!

**Q** What would you hear at a very long **OPERA** about aliens?

**A** Aria 51!

**Q** Why are the people who study the Moon **OPTIMISTS**?

**A** Because they always look on the bright side!

**Q** Why do astronauts regularly visit the **OPTOMETRIST**?

**A** Because they often have stars in their eyes!

HAW-HAW!

**Q** What do you call a fish in **ORBIT**?

**A** A trout-er space!

**Q** What is **ORION'S** Belt?

**A** A huge waist of space!

**Q** Where do alien **OTTERS** come from?

**A** Otter space!

**Q** Why did the cow and the Moon eat **OUT** all the time?

**A** Because their dishes ran away with their spoons!

**Q** What kind of poetry can you find in **OUTER SPACE**?

**A** Uni*verse*!

**Q** Why do astronauts bring **PAINT**, paper, and glue on their trips?

**A** So they can do spacecrafts!

**Q** Where do astronauts **PARK** their spaceships?

**A** Next to parking meteors!

**Q** What's an alien's **PET** called?

**A** An extra-fur-restrial!

**Q** What's a space **PIRATE'S** favorite planet?

**A** M*arrr*s!

LOL!

**Q** What do you call a **PISTACHIO** on a spaceship?

**A** An astro-nut!

**Q** Which cheese goes best on space **PIZZA**?

**A** Mars-arella!

CHORTLE!

**Q** What's an astronaut's favorite **PLACE** to have fun?

**A** Cape carnival!

**Q** Where do **PLANETS** and stars study?

**A** At universe-ity!

**Q** What is the most common **PLANT** in space?

**A** The Venus flytrap!

**Q** What do you call it when someone is **POLITE** in space?

**A** Comet courtesy!

**Q** What award does NASA give to the astronauts that board their spacecraft particularly **QUICKLY**?

**A** The starship enter-prize!

**Q** Which **REINDEER** loves to go to outer space?

**A** Comet!

**Q** What is the most **RELAXING** planet?

**A** Nap-tune!

**Q** What did the alien's **REVIEW** of our solar system say?

**A** "Nothing special . . . one star!"

**Q** What do you call a space **ROBOT** that always takes the longest route?

**A** R2-detour!

SNICKER!

**R**

**Q** Did you hear about the kids who wanted to take a ride in a **ROCKET SHIP**?

**A** They had high hopes!

**Q** What kind of books do **ROMANTIC** aliens like to read?

**A** Love star-ries!

**Q** What's **ROUND**, purple, and orbits the Sun?

**A** Planet of the grapes!

**Q** What do astronauts do if their **ROVER** doesn't fit in a parking spot?

**A** They Moon-ouver it!

**Q** Why should you never be **RUDE** to an alien?

**A** Because you may hurt its feelers!

HAH!

# S

**Q** What is in astronauts' **SANDWICHES**?

**A** Launch-eon meat!

**Q** What do you get if you cross **SANTA CLAUS** with a spaceship?

**A** A U-F-Ho-Ho-Ho!

**Q** Did you hear about the **SATELLITES** that decided to get married?

**A** The wedding wasn't much, but their reception was incredible!

**Q** Why is **SATURN'S** name the best in our solar system?

**A** It has a nice ring to it!

**Q** What did the planet **SAY** to the astronaut?

**A** Nothing—planets can't talk!

GUFFAW!

**Q** Why did the rocket **SCIENTIST** say he stopped working on a project?

**A** He had no comet-ment!

BWAHAHA!

**Q** Why do the planets think the Sun is **SELFISH**?

**A** Because everything revolves around it!

**Q** How do astronauts **SHAVE**?

**A** With a laser blade!

**Q** What did one **SHOOTING STAR** say to the other?

**A** "Pleased to meteor!"

**Q** What do you call it when you mistake dust on the telescope for **SHOOTING STARS**?

**A** Meteor-wrongs!

**Q** How does an alien get its baby to
to go to **SLEEP**?

**A** They rocket!

**Q** What are the **SLOWEST** animals in space?

**A** Snail-iens!

**Q** What are **SMALL** space scientists called?

**A** Astro-gnome-rs!

**Q** What do you call a **SNAKE** in a space suit?

**A** A hiss-tronaut!

**Q** What is an alien's favorite **SOCIAL MEDIA**?

**A** Space-book!

CACKLE!

**S**

**Q** What did the Sun say to the Moon on the day of the **SOLAR ECLIPSE**?

**A** "Looks like it's my night off!"

**Q** How does the **SOLAR SYSTEM** hold up its pants?

**A** With an asteroid belt!

**Q** Why can't you easily describe **SPACE**?

**A** Because it's out of this world!

TEE-HEE!

**Q** What did the **SPACE SHUTTLE** say to the big hole in the Moon?

**A** "See you later, crater!"

**Q** How do they tie things down on the **SPACE STATION**?

**A** With astro knots!

**Q** How many astronauts look good in a **SPACE SUIT**?

**A** Not all of them, but some can rocket!

**Q** What did the alien say as his **SPACECRAFT** passed Mars?

**A** "Red alert! Red alert!"

**Q** Why did the cow go into the **SPACESHIP**?

**A** It wanted to see the Moooooooon!

**Q** Did you hear about the astronaut who didn't believe a rocket could be made of **SPAGHETTI**?

**A** She changed her mind when it flew right pasta!

**Q** What do you call an alien in Times **SQUARE**?

**A** Lost!

HA HA!

**S**

**Q** What do **STARS** say when they apologize to one another?

**A** "I'm starry!"

**Q** What happened to the children who **STAYED** up all night to see where the Sun went?

**A** It finally dawned on them!

HAHAHA!

**Q** Why did the **SUN** go to school?

**A** To get brighter!

**Q** How do you keep a scary Martian in **SUSPENSE**?

**A** I'll tell you later!

**Q** What do you call an alien that lives in a **SWAMP**?

**A** A marsh-in!

**T**

**Q** What do you win for coming second in a space **TALENT** competition?

**A** A constellation prize!

LOL!

**Q** How do you know if you are **TALKING** to an alien disguised as a human?

**A** They they say say everything everything twice twice!

**Q** Why do aliens always spill their **TEA**?

**A** They have flying saucers!

**Q** When do **TEENAGE** rockets get sent to their rooms?

**A** When they have bad altitudes!

**Q** Why did the **TEENAGERS** want to study in a rocket?

**A** They wanted to get higher grades!

**Q** What do false **TEETH** and stars have in common?

**A** They both come out at night!

HAH!

**Q** Why did the **TELESCOPE** operators lose their jobs?

**A** No matter how hard they tried, they just couldn't stay focused!

**Q** Did you hear about the **TELEVISION** show that examines how spacecraft are made?

**A** It's riveting!

**Q** Did you hear that Einstein developed a **THEORY** about space?

**A** And it was about time, too!

**Q** What type of **TINY** alien greetings can scientists detect in space?

**A** Microwaves!

54

**Q** What do aliens spread on their **TOAST**?

**A** Mars-malade!

HE HE!

**Q** What does an astronaut use to keep **TOASTY**?

**A** A space heater!

**Q** Why will space soon become a popular **TOURIST** spot?

**A** The views are breathtaking and will leave you speechless!

**Q** When do you think we'll be able to **TRAVEL** to the Moon?

**A** Lunar or later!

**Q** What do you call a goose who **TRAVELED** to the moon?

**A** A moon-goose!

**Q** What do astronauts enjoying eating as a **TREAT**?

**A** Pie in the sky!

**Q** What do Martians drink when their **TUMMIES** ache?

**A** Ginger ale-ien!

GIGGLE!

**Q** What sound does a space **TURKEY** make?

**A** "Hubble, hubble, hubble!"

**Q** Have you seen the latest **TV** show about black holes?

**A** You'll definitely get sucked in!

**Q** Did you hear about the **TWO** astronauts who adored each other?

**A** It was love at first flight!

**Q** What has a nose but is **UNABLE** to smell?

**A** A space rocket!

**Q** How do you know that the Sun is **UNBLEMISHED**?

**A** Because it always shines!

**Q** Where do you file **UNCATEGORIZED** rocket items?

**A** Under missile-aneous!

**Q** What do you call an **UNDISCOVERED** planet?

**A** I don't know . . . it doesn't have a name yet!

HA HA!

**Q** Did you hear about the scientists who sent a probe to the middle of the **UNIVERSE**?

**A** They discovered the letter *V*!

**Q** Gravity is one of the **UNIVERSE'S** most fundamental forces, but if you remove it, what do you get?

**A** Gravy!

CACKLE!

**Q** Why is being an astronaut such an **UNUSUAL** job?

**A** They are the only people who keep their jobs after they get fired!

**Q** What do baby astronauts want to do when they grow **UP**?

**A** Reach for the stars!

**Q** Why is the law of gravity **USEFUL**?

**A** Because it's easier to pick up something you drop off the floor than the ceiling!

**Q** Why is it **USELESS** to try to tell jokes about satellites?

**A** They always go over people's heads, and they never land!

**Q** Why did Saturn ask for a necklace for **VALENTINE'S** Day?

**A** Because it already had too many rings!

**Q** Which **VEGETABLE** will astronauts never take in a spaceship?

**A** Leeks!

**Q** Which **VEHICLE** did the chicken use to travel into space?

**A** The Starship Henterprise!

**Q** What did **VENUS** say to Earth?

**A** "Ewww, you've got humans!"

**Q** What illness are astronauts most **VULNERABLE** to catching?

**A** The flew!

HAHAHA!

**Q** Why couldn't the astronauts **WALK** when they left the spaceship?

**A** It was too much, too Moon!

**Q** Did you hear what happened when Neil Armstrong first **WALKED** on the Moon?

**A** He didn't understand the gravity of the situation!

**Q** What do aliens use to build **WALLS** on the Moon?

**A** Moonbeams!

**Q** What type of cartoons do aliens enjoy **WATCHING**?

**A** Lunar-toons!

**Q** What do you call a spaceship that drips **WATER**?

**A** A crying saucer!

BWAHAHA!

**Q** What greetings should you send to an astronaut on a mission to find a **WATERING HOLE** on the moon?

**A** "Get well soon!"

**Q** What do aliens wear to **WEDDINGS**?

**A** Space suits!

**Q** Which astronaut did the most **WEIGHT LIFTING**?

**A** Neil Arm*strong*!

**Q** What do you get if you accidently **WHACK** your foot on a rocket?

**A** Missile-toe!

**Q** What do you get when you cross an alien with something **WHITE** and fluffy?

**A** A Martian-mallow!

LOL!

61

**Q** Did you know that space shuttles are made from the same material as **WHITEBOARDS**?

**A** Isn't that re*mark*able!

**Q** What do you call a **WIZARD** in space?

**A** A flying saucer-er!

**Q** Why **WON'T** NASA hire Peter Pan as an astronaut?

**A** Because he'll never, never land!

**Q** What do scientists do when they discover **WORMHOLES**?

**A** They throw their apples away!

**Q** How much is the Moon **WORTH**?

**A** One dollar—because it has four quarters!

CHORTLE!

**Q** What should you do if an astronaut loans you his **X-RAY** telescope and asks if you want to buy it?

**A** Say that you'll look into it!

**Q** How many balls of **YARN** would it take to reach the Moon?

**A** One! One very big ball of yarn!

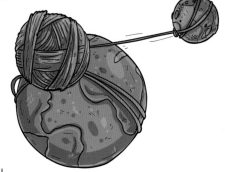

**Q** What's **YELLOW** and white and travels at 1,000 miles per hour?

**A** An astronaut's egg sandwich!

**Q** Why did the patriotic **ZEBRA** go to space?

**A** It was a fan of stars and stripes!

HAHAHA!

**Q** What do astronauts call **ZERO GRAVITY** spaceflights?

**A** Vomit comets!

HA HA!

BWAHAHA!

CACKLE!

HE HE!

LOL!

First American Edition 2022
Kane Miller, A Division of EDC Publishing
Copyright © Green Android Ltd 2022
Illustrated by Vasco Icuza

For information contact:
Kane Miller, A Division of EDC Publishing
5402 S 122nd E Ave
Tulsa, OK 74146
**www.kanemiller.com**
 **www.myubam.com**

Library of Congress Control Number: 2022930296

Printed and bound in Malaysia, June 2022
ISBN: 978-1-68464-520-6

# ALWAYS ARTHUR

For Min
and Jarrad
A. G.

**For a free color catalog describing Gareth Stevens' list
of high-quality children's books, call 1-800-341-3569 (USA)
or 1-800-461-9120 (Canada).**

For more of Arthur's adventures, see
*Who Wants Arthur?*
*Educating Arthur*

**Library of Congress Cataloging-in-Publication Data**

Graham, Amanda, 1961-
  Always Arthur / story by Amanda Graham; pictures by Donna Gynell.
    p. cm.
    Summary: Good-natured Arthur is happy when another dog comes to live in his
household but he soon begins to feel ignored and left out as the new dog seems to
claim all the family's attention.
    ISBN 0-8368-0096-6
    [1. Dogs—Fiction.] I. Gynell, Donna, ill. II. Title.
PZ7.G751664A1     1989
[E]—dc19
                                                      89-4474

North American edition first published in 1990 by

**Gareth Stevens Children's Books**
1555 North RiverCenter Drive, Suite 201
Milwaukee, Wisconsin 53212, USA

First published in Australia by Era Publications.  Text copyright © 1989
by Amanda Graham.  Illustrations copyright © 1989 by Donna Gynell.

Printed in the United States of America

  2 3 4 5 6 7 8 9 96 95 94 93 92 91 90

# ALWAYS ARTHUR

**Story by Amanda Graham**
**Pictures by Donna Gynell**

Gareth Stevens Children's Books
**MILWAUKEE**

When Bonzer suddenly
appeared at the door,
no one was happier than Arthur.
Mr. James put a "lost and found"
notice in the newspaper,
but no one answered it.
So it was decided
that Bonzer should stay.

Arthur thought it was great fun
having Bonzer around.
Now he had someone to chew
old slippers with and to share
his bowl and basket.

In the mornings,
when Arthur and
Melanie ran to the park,
Bonzer joined in.
He always ran fast,
much faster than Arthur.
But Arthur didn't mind.

In the afternoons,
when Arthur and
Melanie played games,
Bonzer joined in.
He always jumped high
to catch the ball,
much higher than Arthur.
But Arthur didn't mind.

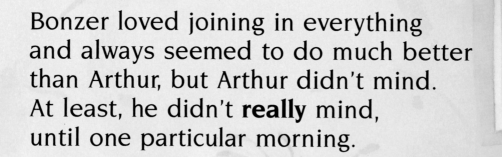

Bonzer loved joining in everything
and always seemed to do much better
than Arthur, but Arthur didn't mind.
At least, he didn't **really** mind,
until one particular morning.

12

13

One particular morning,
Melanie and Bonzer
went to the park without him.
Arthur ran fast and caught up,
only to find that Bonzer was
now Melanie's favorite dog,
and **that** Arthur minded
very much indeed.

So just after dinner,
he found his favorite old slippers
and secretly slid under the fence
and away into the night.

It was not until late in the night
that anyone noticed
Arthur was missing.
"Maybe someone left the gate
open," said Melanie, "or maybe
someone's stolen him."

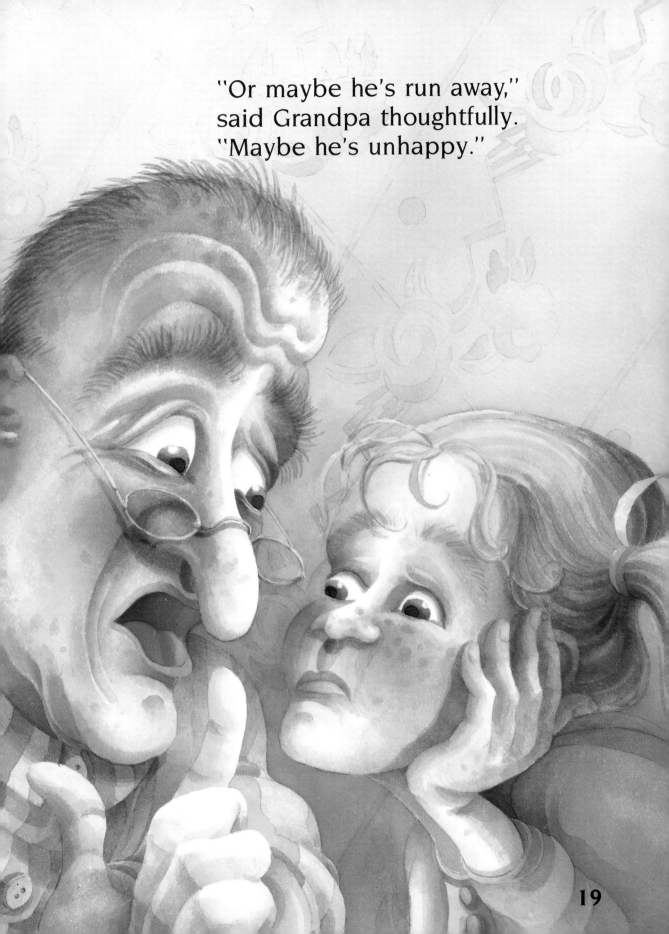

"Or maybe he's run away," said Grandpa thoughtfully. "Maybe he's unhappy."

19

All of a sudden Melanie knew
why Arthur had gone away.
"Come on, Bonzer," she called.
"We have to find Arthur."
Melanie and Bonzer
ran to the park.
"Arthur!" called Melanie.
"Please come home."

But Arthur couldn't hear.
He was too far away.

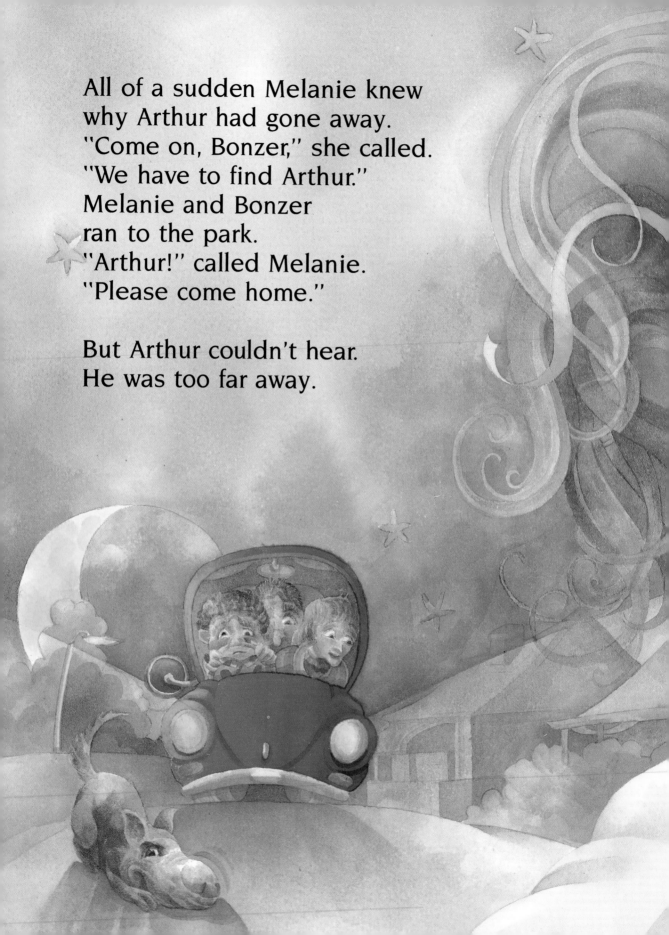

Arthurr
please come

The whole family looked down
every street and lane
for any sign of him.
"Arthur! Please come home!"
they called.

But Arthur couldn't hear.
He was still too far away.
Suddenly Grandpa had an idea.
"I know somewhere we haven't
looked. Let me drive."

Grandpa drove to the main street
and turned the corner near
Mrs. Humber's Pet Shop.
"There he is, Grandpa,
in front of the shop!"
shouted Melanie.
"There's Arthur!"

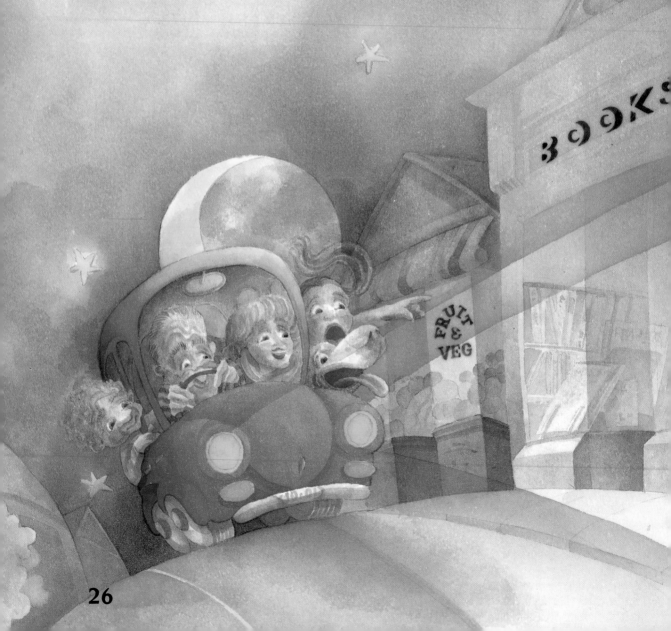

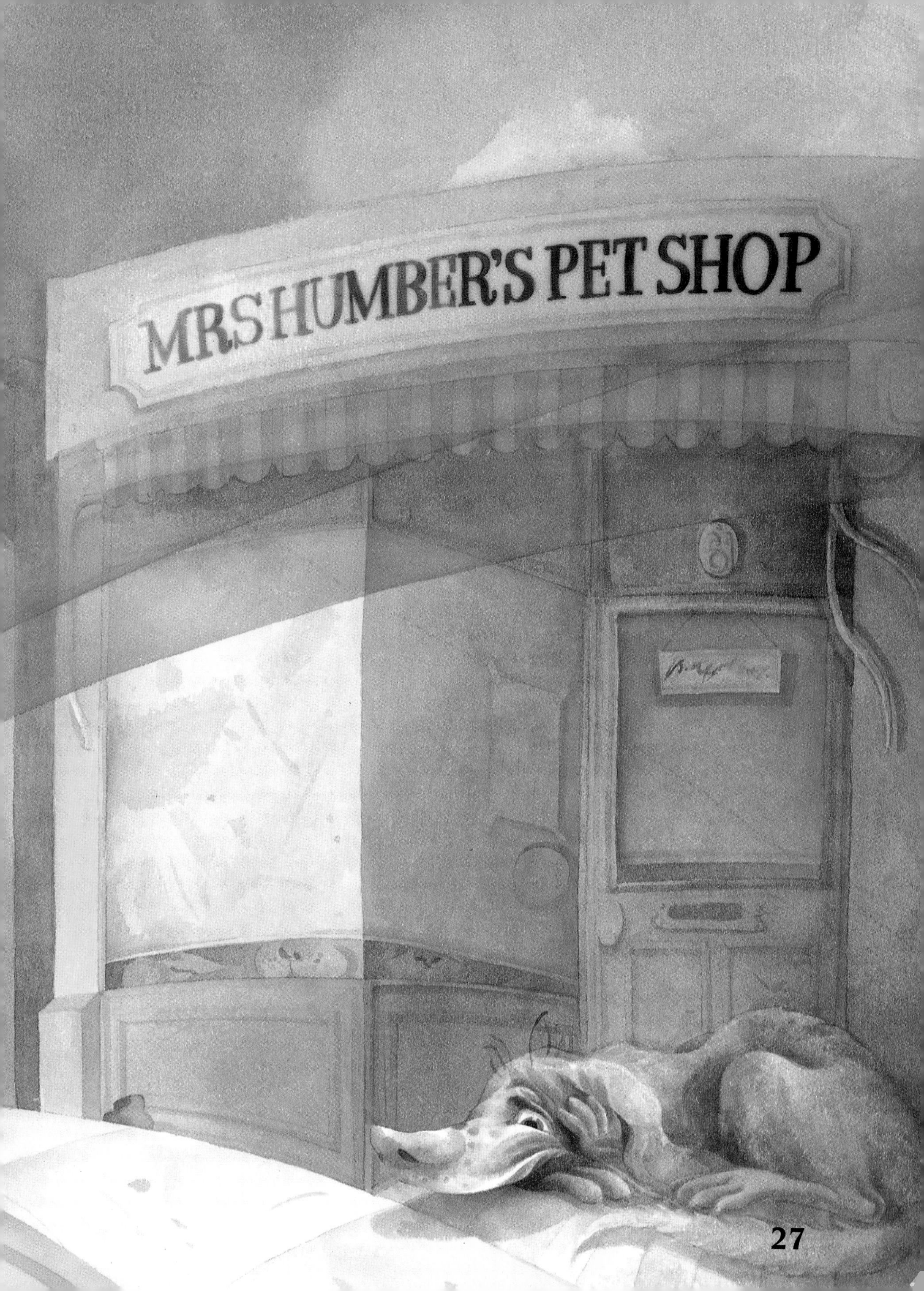
MRS HUMBER'S PET SHOP

Grandpa stopped the car.
Melanie jumped out,
ran to Arthur, and
gave him the biggest,
warmest, cuddliest hug ever.
"Please come home.
I love you," said Melanie
as she squeezed him tightly.
"I will always love you,
Arthur. . .

. . .always!"